Working the Party

FreeUse Erotica Story

Lacey Cross

Twisted Rose Publishing

ISBN 13: 978-1-960162-06-9 (Paperback edition)

Editor, Adam Gaffen

Contents

Chapter 1

The first time my husband, Mark, dared me to fuck another man was about three months ago. It all started so innocently...

"Hey, baby? You know how we used to play truth or dare?"

Mark just returned from the grocery store and I'm helping unload the bags from the back of our SUV. I grin at him as I pick up the last bag.

"Of course I do. We had to stop playing because you only ever picked truth and I ran out of things to ask."

"Hmm... that's not how I remember it." He slams the trunk door shut and hits the key fob to make sure it's locked. "I think it was you who kept choosing dare, and I ran out of things to dare you to do."

"Nooo, that's so not how it happened."

As we haul the bags into the kitchen and start unloading, we're still play-fighting over who is right. I hold my ground and deny I was the reason the game stopped. I mean, he can barely find his work shoes each day. There's no way he remembers something that happened years ago.

I'm in the pantry organizing the canned goods when he calls out, "Fine, but for right now — Truth or Dare."

Oh, jeez. He knows how this is going to end. I'll bet he's planned something for me.

"Dare!"

His laugh is louder than I expect. Oh great, now I know he has something in mind for me.

"I dare you to fuck another guy while I watch."

What's this?

I stop organizing the pantry and spend a few moments imagining getting railed by another guy while Mark watches. My entire body lights with desire, and my panties grow damp.

Jesus, get a grip, Jennifer. There's no way Mark really wants this.

"Sure. Let's go ask Gary next door if he'll fuck me. I'm sure Millie won't mind."

When I walk out of the pantry, Mark grins at me. "I told you they were fucking in the garage the other night. I think Millie has a tight leash on him. He seemed plenty satisfied."

I heard about the garage fucking from Millie as well. They attended a wedding, and she fucked the entire band after the reception. When they came home, Gary took her against the wall in their garage. I got a dirty thrill from hearing the juicy details, but I knew it was never something that Mark would want. My guy is vanilla in the bedroom and I'm fine with that.

Blowing my crazy hubby a kiss, I take another bag into the pantry and put more cans away, figuring I'd called his bluff.

"See, guess you're out of luck. There's no one for me to fuck."

"What about Ian?"

Ian? The mental image of fucking his massive red-haired beast of a friend sears my brain. The can of corn in my hand tumbles to the floor and rolls under a wire shelving unit.

Oh god, he's not really wanting me to fuck Ian, is he?

I pop my head back out of the pantry to so I can see his face.

He's dead serious.

My pussy buzzes as my breath quickens, but I'm still not ready to admit I like this idea. He's pranking me. Once I agree to it, he'll tease me forever about wanting to ride his friend's thick cock.

Not that I really know how big it is, but I've heard rumors.

I don't want to be in the pantry having this conversation, so I move into the kitchen before answering him. When I do, I try to make light of it.

"You're silly. Ian wouldn't want to fuck me. With that red hair and beard, he's probably got women drooling after him."

Ian is quite sexy. Okay, maybe more than quite. Incredibly? Amazingly? Punches all my buttons? Does he really have a gigantic cock? Mark is adequate. More important, he knows how to use it, but I've always been curious what a guy sporting an anaconda in his pants could do to me.

"I know Ian would. He jokingly asked if I would share you."

Uh.. what? I stop moving as my brain processes this new information.

Mark sees he befuddled me, and he laughs again. "Yeah. He was at his cousin's bachelor party in a cabin in the mountains and a stripper came by and fucked all the guys. She was wearing a wedding ring, so he's been getting off to thoughts of fucking married women ever since."

A splash of wetness hits my panties and my nipples harden.

Mmm, oh yeah, I'd fuck Ian all right.

But I don't want to seem too eager.

I give a casual, "Yeah, okay. I'd fuck him if you really wanted me to."

Please say yes. Please say yes.

"Ian's birthday is this weekend and his friends reserved the back room at the Dancing Dog Beer Garden for a party. Want to be his present?"

The name of the bar makes me giggle, but I straighten my face and try to act serious. Even a little reluctant.

"Uh... sure."

CHAPTER 2

From then until the party, I was crazy turned on. Mark and I fucked on practically every surface of our house. It was barely enough to take the edge off.

I scheduled a wax a few days before so I'd be smooth skinned and soft in all the right places. On the morning of the party, I pampered myself with a spa day. I chose a deep red polish for my mani-pedi that matches my red tank top and spiked high heels. I decided to slut it up for the party, so I'm wearing daisy dukes that barely cover my ass, and I didn't bother with a bra. My breasts are generous and pert enough that I can get away without one. Mostly, I want Ian to see my nipples. To finish my look, my long, brown hair is in a ponytail, so it won't be a mess after Ian gives me a good fucking.

I know I look hot, and I'm feeling sexy. I'm ready to strut my stuff and make all the men drool.

By the time we arrive at the bar, the party is in full swing. The front of the house is packed. Mark knows the bartender, who waves us to the backroom. Right before we go in, Mark grips my forearm to stop me.

"Wait a minute."

My stomach jumps with excitement and I'm eager to see Ian's reaction, but I force myself to pay attention to Mark. This is Mark's fantasy. While I'm fully on board with the plan and I want to do it, I also want to make sure Mark gets attention and has a fun time.

"Hmm, yes?"

He pulls me into his arms for a kiss. Our tongues dance briefly and my pussy clenches with need. When he breaks off the kiss, he nibbles on my neck. Desire warms me. I love him so much.

His breath is warm against my ear when he speaks. "I'm giving you the freedom to fuck whoever you want to tonight. It doesn't have to be Ian."

Whoa.

I pull back so I can look him in the eyes. "But I want to fuck Ian."

He grins and gives me a quick peck on my nose. "I know you do, Baby. I'm just saying you don't have to fuck only Ian. You can have all the cock you want."

I eye him skeptically. My vanilla guy offering me multiple cocks? What does he get out of this?

"What if I go in there and fuck twenty guys?"

He laughs. "That might be difficult, since I know only five guys were invited."

I wonder if he knows me at all? Get me horny enough and I'll start pulling guys from the bar into the back room. I was quite the slut in college. First girl invited to every frat party, and I hardly ever said no. But that was years ago. I've only been with Mark since we got married.

"You know what I mean. Do you really want to see me fucking a bunch of men?"

He looks down at the floor and shrugs. "If we're only going to do this one time, might as well make it good. Right?"

A faint pink tint stains his cheeks. Oh holy hell, my husband DOES want to watch me get railed by a bunch of guys. He's embarrassed by wanting it. Snuggling close to him, I wrap my arms around his neck and tug on his hair to make him look at me.

"Thank you, my love. If the mood strikes me, I'll take you up on the offer... assuming the guys want to fuck me."

The way my dang slutty cunt is buzzing, the mood is definitely going to strike me. Just the thought of having multiple men again is enough to make me a needy whore and willing to open my legs for anyone in the room. Like Mark said, if this is the only time we're going to do this. I'm going to make it good.

"I told them you had permission to fuck whomever you wanted. You can say they were enthusiastic about the idea."

Ohhhh.

My brain blips out for a minute while he kisses me again. As I press against him, I can feel his hard cock through his jeans. I'm able to think again, and my panties grow damp. Hot damn, I didn't know my husband had such a filthy fantasy.

This is awesome.

"Baby, are you ready for this?"

I'm practically vibrating with excitement and nod eager-
ly. "Oh yeah, let's do it!"

CHAPTER 3

When we enter the backroom, all conversation stops and five pairs of eyes swivel towards us. The men sit at a round table. The wooden surface is covered with empty shot glasses, baskets of pub finger foods, and half-empty pitchers of beer.

Ian, the birthday boy, is the largest of the guys. With the red hair and beard, he's hard to miss. He's holding a mug of beer, and his hands distract me for a moment. My god, they're huge. He could probably fit my entire breast into his palm, an impressive feat since I'm not small chested.

I was already buzzing from the anticipation of fucking Ian, but I get an extra shot of lust when I see the rest of the group. The other four are attractive, in an average middle age sort of way. I mean, I wouldn't toss any of them out of my bed for eating cookies. They all have beards, which strikes me as funny. This isn't no-shave November. Do they have a weird pact going on?

Not that I care. I love men with beards. They're able to tickle me in all the right places.

No one speaks. All five continue to stare at me. I feel my face heating.

Fuck it. I'll get us started.

I dig deep and channel my college-age slutty self and sashay towards the table.

"I hope you all brought your A game. My husband wants to watch you all fuck me hard."

Maybe a little exaggeration there, since Mark never said he wanted it hard. That's all on me.

Ian smiles. His eyes twinkle as he raises his glass in a toast. "To a great birthday!"

I can get down with that sentiment. Grabbing one of the half-finished beers from the table, I take a long swig before raising it towards Ian.

"Here's to making it memorable. Now." I put the glass down and meet every single pair of eyes in turn. "Who wants to fuck me?"

The guys laugh as Ian stands up.

"Come here, you sexy little minx. Let's give the boys a show."

All it took was a little push, and now this is moving fast, but I've been wanting his thick cock all day. He can bend me over the table right now and I'd just moan like the greedy slut I am.

My legs are rubbery as I circle the table. As I pass each guy, I run my hands along their shoulders, letting my fingernails graze the backs of their necks. I get the insane urge to play duck-duck-goose, and the tag-you're-it guy is the one who gets to fuck me.

When I get close to Ian, I stop within arm's reach. I came this far; he's going to have to make the next move. With a little guidance from me. Now that I've got it in my head I want him to bend me over and fuck me, I'm going to do whatever I can to make him do exactly that.

He'll think it was his idea.

He steps forward and reaches for my waistband, but I slip out of his grasp to turn my back to him, pressing against him. His fingers glide over my ass. Pleasure zips through me and I wiggle my butt against his hand. I discover the material of the daisy dukes is annoyingly thick. I want his warm palm on my bare ass.

He runs his hands down and along my inner thighs. I spread my legs to give him better access as my pussy buzzes happily.

Jesus. I haven't even been here five minutes and already his hand is between my legs. I'm such a slut.

But I'm a happy slut.

He cups my mound in his hand. I arch my back in delight and thrust my hips towards him.

Dammit, I need these shorts off.

He holds onto my hip with one hand while he rubs my jeans-covered pussy with the other. Leaning down, he whispers in my ear. "Are you going to be a good little toy and let us all fuck you?"

His breath tickles me and I'm momentarily tongue tied. I nod my agreement before letting out a breathy "Yes."

"Then take off your shorts, slut."

Perfection. Ohhh, yes. I move my hand to my waistband, idly wondering if Mark told him how much I love being called a slut? Then I freeze. Wait, where is Mark?

A quick peek around the room shows me Mark sitting in a chair a few feet from the table. He's staring at me and lust shoots straight to my clit from the intensity of his gaze.

Holy shit! My brain goes fuzzy and I'm hit by a deep yearning to be drenched in cum in front of Mark. I regaled him with all the slutty stories from my younger years, but he's never seen me act that way. It's time for him to see how filthy his wife really is.

I unbutton my shorts with shaking hands, and wiggle them down my thighs.

Glancing over my shoulder, I raise an eyebrow at Ian. "Panties too?"

Ian runs his hand over the satin red material before giving me a husky, "Yes."

My pussy throbs with excitement and my clit aches. Good. This is going to get me fucked quicker. I shimmy out of the wet panties and step out carefully so my heels don't get tangled in the material. As I'm about to toe them aside, I change my mind and only push the shorts out of my way. I reach down to grab my panties, ball them up, and aim at Mark.

"I've got a present for you, my love."

I hurl them at him. Mark catches them easily and moves them to his nose. He inhales deeply before tucking them into his pocket. He looks a little dazed as he focuses back on me.

Oh god, he just sniffed my arousal for another man. Okay, that's fucking hot. I almost ask him if he's still good with this, but the bulge in his jeans says he's enjoying everything.

I'm naked from the waist down and ready for action, but it's not enough. I pull my tank top over my head and let it fall to the floor. The guys around the table can see my front. The closest one licks his lips while he stares at my breasts. It might seem weird that no one introduced me to the other guys, but I prefer it this way. I want to be used by a bunch of strangers, and this hits the kink safely. Mark is such an amazing husband to organize this.

Ian reaches around and cups my breasts. He's flush against my back and his erection presses against my ass. When he pulls at my nipples, I moan from pleasure.

God, just fuck me already.

As he uses his massive paws to play with my breasts, I can't help teasing him.

"What do you think?"

He laughs. "I can't decide if I like your tits or your ass better."

I grind my ass against him. "Well, I think I know which one you prefer."

"You think so, do you?"

"Yep. And if you're a good boy, I might let you have it."

He takes a step back. "I can just take my birthday present." Before I can say anything, he spins me and presses my shoulders to the surface of the table.

Ohhh, fuck yes. He's playing perfectly into my hand.

Two guys grab baskets of food and push them aside so I don't smash them. Not that I care. I'm about to get what I want.

A sharp slap on my ass makes me squeak. "Hey!"

"Jennifer, you remind me of someone." Ian's voice has a gravelly tone that sets my pussy tingling.

"Oh, yeah?"

He gives me another hard spank and wetness trickles down my inner thigh. Damn, I love being spanked.

"Yeah. Did Mark tell you how I had a freeuse slut in the mountains?" He rains hard smacks on my ass, alternating cheeks.

"Yes.... God, yes." Fuuuuck, this is amazing. If he keeps this up, I'll be begging him to fuck me however he wants.

A delicious pain vibrates through my core the longer he spanks me. Each hit sinks me further into a submissive state, dulls the sharpness of the sting, and turns it to pleasure. I close my eyes and drift on a sea of euphoria. I'm so mentally fuzzy, I don't notice he's stopped spanking me until the tip of his cock presses against my wet folds.

"Do you want to know how the night in the cabin ended?"

I open my eyes and moan out a breathy "yes." I want to cry out and beg him to fuck me while he finishes the story, but I'm distracted by the guy sitting next to me. He's staring at me with fire in his eyes. I can tell he wants to fuck me hard. Will they all just pound into me and use me? Am I even going to come?

Ohhhh, god.

My nipples harden painfully. I clutch the edges of the table to hold myself steady in case Ian rams into me and starts going to town. If I don't find pleasure with these guys, I know Mark will take care of me when we get home... unless he's crazed with lust.

Fuck. He already is. What if I don't come tonight?

Ian rubs the tip of his cock against my clit. I moan and wiggle my ass. I want to know what a monster cock feels like inside me again. It's been years since I've had one bigger than average.

He slides the length along my slit before sinking into me. As he presses in slowly, he stretches me out, inch by agonizing inch, as pings of bliss explode in my brain.

Shiiiiit, he's huge.

Once Ian bottoms out, he remains buried in me and continues the story.

"After the freeuse slut showed up, all the guys fucked her. Then we used her mouth."

I know all of this from Mark, but I don't tell him. My head spins when he pulls out fully. He fills me again before stopping.

"We fucked her until she was mindless. She was such a beautiful mess, all covered in cum when we were done with her."

Oh, fuck. That's hot.

"But the best part of the night? I was the first and the last guy to fuck her"

Why is he telling me this? I can't think with his cock inside me. I squirm, trying to get him to thrust. Jesus, can't he see I need him to fuck me?

"Since this is my birthday. I'm going to do the same to you. I'm going to use you all I want. You're my freeuse gift from your husband."

Hold on. My husband gave me to him? Like I'm a piece of property?

My pussy clenches around his cock and my entire body flushes. Oh fuck, why is this hot?

He pulls out, grabs hold of my hips, and slams into me.

I scream.

"Oooh my god!" My eyes close again as he pummels my pussy.

Jesus Christ. Mark better be enjoying this show. This is fucking fabulous.

The table shakes and the glasses and plates rattle from the force of him jackhammering into me. Every thrust sends me reeling higher. I tighten my grip on the edge of the table to keep from being knocked around like a rag doll.

Ian wraps my ponytail around his fist and pulls, forcing me to lift my head. I stare straight ahead and realize Mark is right in my line of sight. He's enjoying me being used, stroking himself through his pants, his eyes hooded with desire. I whimper from a spike of bliss.

Ian pumps into me relentlessly. "Is this what you wanted, my freeuse slut?"

I pant out, "Harder! Fuck me harder!"

He pulls back and slaps my ass with his other hand. "You think I'm going easy on you, slut? You're my toy to do with as I wish. So get ready for it because I'm going to fuck your brains out."

Ian's dirty talk is filthier than anything Mark ever says to me. Every time he calls me a slut, a part of my brain pings. I am a slut, and these guys can do whatever they want to me tonight. I'll love everything.

My pussy throbs, and I'm aching for him to fill me with his cum. It's been years since I've had anyone else's jizz inside me, and tonight I want all I can get. The idea of dripping with all their cum spirals me closer to orgasm. I'm just a dirty whore that needs it.

Ian's fist grips my hair tighter as he continues slamming into me, grunting in time with each thrust. My thigh muscles tense as bliss ripples through me.

Ohhhh, I'm going to come!

He growls and increases his pace, and I can tell he's getting close by how he's moaning. He pushes in deep, slapping his balls against my swollen clit with each powerful lunge. When he speeds up and fucks me, every quick thrust hits an amazing spot with the head of his cock. My entire body tenses as I dangle over the precipice, and it barely registers that I'm begging.

"Oh god, don't stop, don't stop, don't... ohhhhhhh, YES!"

A sharp whack against my pussy tips me over the edge. I cry out and convulse around his cock. In a few strokes, Ian moans loudly and explodes. His hot seed floods my pussy while I shudder and milk his cock, hungry to claim all his cum. His strokes slow until finally he stops.

When he pulls out of me, I moan from the emptiness. My hands ache from gripping the table so hard as I release them and flex my fingers. Ian reaches down to rub my throbbing pussy, and I whimper as he fingers my sensitive clit.

"She's warmed up. Who's next?"

CHAPTER 4

I close my eyes and drift as the guy to my right pushes his chair back with a loud scrape.

"Me."

His voice is deeper than I expect. It gives me a pleasant buzz, but I'm drained of energy. He'll have to fuck me like this.

Another chair scrapes the floor behind me as the guy grabs my hips. He pulls me off the table straight onto his cock. Ohhhh fuck. So much for me laying around.

He's not as big as Ian, but he's not small either. He stretches my pussy walls and heat spreads inside me. A burst of energy shakes off my lingering lethargy and I'm ready for this.

Giddy up!

This is so damn slutty. Knowing I'm riding another dude's cock in front of the others causes a wave of humiliation to roll over me. I feel the flush on my face and close my eyes. I absolutely love being a filthy slut and taking a bunch of cocks, but part of reason I love it is this right here, these guys treating me like I'm a piece of ass to be used. It gets me off more than the cock inside me does. Mark being here to witness my debasement makes it worse in the most delicious way.

This is what I crave.

Digging his fingers into my hips, the guy forces me up and down his shaft in a steady pace. I spread my legs so they're outside his legs and play with my nipples while bouncing on his lap. The bliss builds in my core again as he and I find the perfect rhythm. Being on top I enjoy the illusion of control, and he moans as I roll my hips.

"You're gorgeous," he whispers in my ear.

My heart pounds at his compliment. Dang, I didn't expect praise.

"Thank you." I grind harder into him and look over my shoulder at him. "Do you want to come?"

He laughs and then groans. "God, yes."

"Then fuck me and fill me up."

Not that he needed permission, or was going to wait until I came, but my words spur him into a frenzy. His grip becomes punishing, and he slams me against him so hard and fast my entire body jerks. I release my breasts and they swing free as he uses me. I'm moaning incoherently as another orgasm threatens to consume me, but I can tell it won't hit fast enough.

He keeps pounding into me, whispering dirty things into my ear.

"You're such a fucking slut and your pussy feels so good."

Ohhh, fuck.

"I'm going to come. Are you ready?"

My mind is fuzzy, so all I can do is moan, "Yes, fuck me hard. I need it."

The room spins and my vision blurs as his thrusts become erratic. Oh fuck, I'm so close to coming. Please, please, please let it hit before he finishes.

"Get ready. Here it comes!"

I don't know if he's talking to me or himself, but I cry out when his hot cum spurts inside me.

My whole body shudders with each pulse of his cock as he unloads ropes of his sticky goodness. My body quivers from the denied orgasm and I hold in a whimper of distress.

Oh Fuuuuuck, I didn't come. And without the friction of movement, there's no way I will. Mark had better make this evening end with an orgasm. This torture is wonderful, but I need to come so badly.

When he's finished with me, he lifts me off, slaps my ass, and bends me over the table again.

"Who's next with our freeuse slut?"

It's an endless second before someone speaks up.

"I am."

As the guys change positions, I lift my head and squint at Mark through my fog of lust. He's still stroking his cock with a soft smile on his face.

That's all I needed to see.

I drop my head to the table again and turn so my cheek is against the cool surface. My pussy throbs. I wish it was Mark who was going to fuck me next, but the show isn't over yet.

Another guy walks behind me and runs his hands over my ass.

"Such a pretty ass. Can I fuck it?"

What?

My eyes fly open and I look for Mark's reaction. I didn't consider this possibility, though my pussy clenches at the thought. Yeah, I'm not surprised she wants it.

Mark laughs. "Only if you have lube. I didn't bring any."

The guys around the table grumble and joke about not keeping emergency lube on them, and I relax back into the table with a pang of regret.

Damn. I sort of wanted it.

Someday—soon—I'll tempt Mark into fucking my ass and imagine I'm back here.

When I feel the guy's cock probing my entrance, I groan at the bliss that immediately consumes me. It's been so many years since I've had multiple men in one night, I almost forgot how incredible it is. Even if you don't come with one guy, the next one is likely to get you there.

Or the next.

He slams into me, and I gasp at the sudden invasion. Holy fuck, this guy is long. He's not super thick, but he's reaching a spot deep inside me that the other two missed. My pussy squeezes around his length.

"Damn, you're so wet," he says as he pulls out, only to thrust back in again vigorously.

I hear myself chanting, "Yes," as the pleasure builds in layers.

My legs shake as my climax approaches.

Oh god, this is going to be a big one.

He's whacking against my pussy at a brutal pace and hitting that wonderful spot deep inside me with every thrust. When my orgasm hits, it's like I'm struck by lightning. My back arches and I scream out, "YES!" as a sharp pleasure races to my fingers and my toes.

Knowing I came tips him over the edge. He groans, "You dirty whore," as his seed spurts inside me. I squeeze him tight and take everything he can give me.

When he's finished, I collapse forward on the table with my head on my arms. Tiny aftershocks of pleasure run through my body and I giggle. He's right. I am a dirty whore.

Wait, how many men are left? I think that was the third guy, so two more... I think. Fuck, how did I lose track already?

Right. Being fucked silly. Messes with math.

Another guy speaks up. "I want to fuck her mouth. Dan, do you want her pussy while I do that?"

Ohhhh.... yes, please.

"Yeah, I want a piece of that sweet pussy." Well, at least I know one name now. Dan.

I love having two guys at once, and it's a common fantasy while Mark fucks me.

The guys help me from the table to the floor, making sure we're in a spot where Mark can see all the action. I consider kicking my heels off, but it seems sluttier to wear them. Neither of them are rough with me, but being manhandled and moved into their position makes me feel like their fucktoy.

It's glorious.

A guy kneels in front of me, and all I can see is his thick cock sticking out from his jeans. He didn't even bother to pull his pants down.

He's going to regret that. My new goal is to be so messy he ends up with a wet patch on the front of his jeans when I'm done with him.

"Suck my cock."

"Mmm, yes," I purr and lean forward so he can push it between my lips.

He's long and smooth, and his pre-cum tastes so damn good. Throwing myself onto his cock, I slobber all over him. I want his shaft nice and wet so I don't swallow the excess saliva. His moans are loud, and I gurgle happily around his shaft when wetness drips from my mouth.

Dan probes my pussy with the head of his cock. I moan around the shaft in my mouth as the cock behind me sinks into me. He isn't gentle, jackhammering into my pussy without giving me time to adjust to his invasion.

I'm spit-roasted, and a dark twist of desire coils in me. I'm not sure I want to come again tonight. If they all fuck me and leave me a wet, needy mess, I'd feel more like I was used... which is exactly what I want.

I don't realize that Mark moved from his chair until I sense someone kneel beside me. He leans over and whispers in my ear.

"You love being a slut, don't you?"

Oh... my... god.

I gurgle, "Yes," around the cock fucking my mouth and try to nod my head.

"You enjoy being filled with cocks. Used like the slut you are. Don't deny it."

Who is this person I married? Mark's degrading me is fucking me up more than the two guys filling my holes. I try to say Yes again, but I'm not sure he hears it.

The guy in my mouth speeds up. Dan, behind me, is plowing into me so hard it's forcing the cock further down my throat.

"You love being my slut. Don't you?"

Fuck, yes… yes, I do. All I can do is moan as the two guys use me.

Mark runs his hand along my side, tickling me, and I shiver. When he plays with a nipple and pinches it hard, my pussy clenches around the cock inside it and I almost come.

Fuuuck.

I'm whimpering around the cock in my mouth. When Mark smacks my tit, my body shudders from the strength of my orgasm. My loud cry is muffled, and I convulse as waves of pleasure wash over me.

The cock in my mouth spasming is the only warning before he floods my throat with cum. He holds my head and gives tiny thrusts as he unloads. Excess cum and saliva drip along his shaft. I'm so far gone, I can't tell if any is getting on his jeans. I sure hope so.

I'm so focused on the guy in front me I almost forget Dan hasn't come yet. He gives one final hard thrust and growls as he explodes. I'm reeling as the guy pulls out of my mouth, and Dan holds onto my hips and grinds against me as he finishes his last blasts into my pussy.

When he pulls out, I'm almost limp. Mark moves in front of me. I cling to him and shake.

"I love you so much, Jennifer. You're fucking amazing."

I look into his sparkling eyes and smile. My brain is too wooly for words yet.

"I'm not done with our freeuse slut."

What's this? I turn my head to see Ian sitting in a chair. He's stroking that impressive cock.

"I've got one last load to blow in her mouth."

Mark pets my cheek. "Guess you better get to it."

Excitement buzzes in my stomach, and I realize I'm not ready for this to be over.

Mark kisses me deeply before letting me go. I wiggle my ass at my husband as I crawl over to take the last load. Ian shifts his legs wider so I can kneel between them. I contemplate his monster of a cock. I'm not sure how to go about this.

But Ian does.

He reaches down, takes my hand, and guides it to his shift. I stroke up and down slowly, appreciating the contours of his veins and soft skin. He's warm and heavy in my hand, and I grip him tighter, enjoying how he pulses against my palm. His cock is so large it's like a toy. I could play with him all night, but I know Mark also needs attention. I'm desperate to get home and get fucked by my husband.

I lean forward slightly and trail kisses along his thigh, heading straight for his cock. I don't think he expected that, and his thigh muscles twitch under my cum-covered lips. Once I reach his cock, I see he's so big I'll have to stretch my lips around the head.

When I lick the underside, I know from his loud moan he likes it. I swirl my tongue around the tip, focusing on the sensitive spot underneath. He's more responsive than some men I've blown. It's great when a guy clearly enjoys what I'm doing. I let saliva drip down his cock to lubricate him, and I rub his cock to spread it around. Once he's wet enough, I get brave and slowly lower my mouth, letting him sink inside.

I'm not sure I've ever had someone this big inside my throat, but I'm going to give him the best blowjob I can. I bob my head as I swirl my tongue along his shaft. Using my hand, I stroke whatever can't fit in my mouth. Ian groans and twitches. He's loving what I'm doing.

I speed up, and the head of his cock hits the back of my throat. I take him down as far as I can, relaxing my throat so I don't gag, and suck on him. My only goal is to get him off. I want him to have a birthday to remember.

I work my mouth down the length of him, alternating with short and long bobs of my head. He doesn't know what to expect. I take as much of his length as I can, and he rewards me with a long moan. He slides his hands around my head, holding loosely as I continue my ministrations to his cock.

He tenses up, and I take advantage of the moment. Sucking him in as deep as I can, I fondle his balls. When he hits the back of my throat, his body jerks and he erupts.

He groans and holds my head firmly as he shudders with his release. Copious amounts of cum hit my tongue and coat my mouth. I can't swallow it all fast enough and some spills out of the corners of my mouth. When he's finished, I swallow what remains and then lick his softening shaft to help clean him up. He is the birthday boy, after all.

When he's as clean as I can get him, I sit back on my heels.

I'm a mess.

A mixture of cum and my juices drips out of me. The room spins a little as emotions rush through me. I can't believe how much I missed the feeling of being a complete whore. But it's different now. This time I'm Mark's whore. He wanted this just as much as I did.

I'm sitting close enough to Ian that he can touch me. He cups my face and rubs my cheek to get my attention.

"Thank you, Jennifer. This was an amazing gift."

His thanks pull me out of my thoughts, and I feel more like myself.

I grin at him. "You're welcome."

Ian's words spur everyone else to chime in with their thanks.

Mark helps me stand. He finds my shorts and I hold him while he helps me get each foot into the leg hole. Somehow we manage it without falling or getting tangled in my heels. As he's zipping up the shorts, I realize we're missing an important piece of clothing.

"Panties?"

"Nope, you don't need them."

Heh. I suppose not. These shorts need a good washing before I wear them again. Mark retrieves my tank top from the floor and I slip it on. As it settles over my breasts, my sensitive nipples ache.

Mark kisses me softly and murmurs. "Let's get out of here. It's my turn now."

Anticipation lights my blood. I'm ready for my husband to fuck me.

CHAPTER 5

We don't even make it to the car. As soon as we're out-side, Mark drags me around the back of the building. He's crazed and seeing him this needy for me makes this entire night worth it. I unbuckle my shorts and push them down while he fumbles with his pants to free his cock.

As soon as it's out, he grabs my thigh and I let my high heel fall off as he pulls my leg up. I grasp his shoulders and wrap my leg around him as he slams his cock into me.

Pleasure assaults my senses, and I gasp as he pounds away at my pussy. Each thrust knocks me against the wall.

It's awesome.

"God, baby. I love you. It was so hot watching all those men fuck you."

Ohhh. My head spins as Mark keeps talking.

"You were like a goddess of cock. And all mine."

This might sound stupid to anyone listening, but him calling me a goddess of cock pings something in my brain.

I pleasured five men tonight, and my husband is about to come as well.

Yeah, I am a fucking goddess.

We both start moving faster, and I can tell I'm about to come. I'm breathing hard, my thighs quivering as he drills into me. He kisses me, and our tongues tangle together. My body tightens. An extra hard ram from him tips me over the edge. I cry out as bliss wracks my body. My pussy throbs and euphoria blasts through me. Mark is right there with me, grunting in pleasure as he erupts. I cling to him as he unloads into my pussy.

When we both come down from our high, my body is limp. My knees buckle, but Mark holds me up. I can't think straight for a minute until the pleasure fades.

Holy fuck. That was amazing.

He supports me until he can tell I'm coherent enough to stand on my own. Even then he helps steady me.

"Let's get home, baby. I want to shower with you and pamper your sore bits."

My pussy twitches and I smile. Oh yeah, she's sore and probably going to be even more so tomorrow. Such a delicious soreness... but he can pamper me if he wants. It's only proper. I am a goddess of the cock.

I take his hand and we walk to the car together.

Fuck, I love my husband.

I hope he wants to do this again someday.

The End

can become a **mindless toy** as they experience the ultimate pleasure... over and over again.

Includes:

Taking Them All This hotwife hopes that when her husband said anyone and anywhere, it includes multiple men.

Borrowing The Bride This first time hotwife didn't expect her wedding night to include more than just the groom.

Pleasing The Crowd This bridesmaid wants to pretend she's the bride and shared with a group of men for some filthy fun.

Gratifying The Guys This bridesmaid isn't the bimbo everyone assumes she is, and she's going to get exactly what she wants... to be shared, used, and turned into a toy for the night.

Auditioning The Band This hotwife didn't know that her husband had a dirty fantasy of sharing her. When a joke about multiple men turns serious, her husband knows just the guys for the job – his best friend's band.

These short stories contain graphic depictions of sex between consenting adults and features elements of hotwife, multiple men, and freeuse, and BDSM. Reader discretion advised.

About Lacey Cross

I'm mainly a writer who got bored during the pandemic and turned to erotica out of desperation. I found out I love the creativity and challenge of self-publishing sexy stories.

I write a variety of kinks, but most are wife sharing with a touch of BDSM power control.

Connect with me at:

https://lacey-cross.com/